The Meadow Vale Ponies

MULBERRY

FOR SALE

ALSO AVAILABLE:

Mulberry and the Summer Show

COMING SOON:

Mulberry to the Rescue!
Mulberry Gets up to Mischief

MULBERRY

FOR SALE

Che Golden

OXFORD
UNIVERSITY PRESS

OXFORD
UNIVERSITY PRESS

Great Clarendon Street, Oxford OX2 6DP

Oxford University Press is a department of the University of Oxford.
It furthers the University's objective of excellence in research, scholarship,
and education by publishing worldwide in

Oxford New York

Auckland Cape Town Dar es Salaam Hong Kong Karachi
Kuala Lumpur Madrid Melbourne Mexico City Nairobi
New Delhi Shanghai Taipei Toronto

With offices in

Argentina Austria Brazil Chile Czech Republic France Greece
Guatemala Hungary Italy Japan Poland Portugal Singapore
South Korea Switzerland Thailand Turkey Ukraine Vietnam

Oxford is a registered trade mark of Oxford University Press
in the UK and in certain other countries

British Library Cataloguing in Publication Data

Data available

ISBN: 978-0-19-273468-6

3 5 7 9 10 8 6 4 2

Printed in Great Britain

Paper used in the production of this book is a natural,
recyclable product made from wood grown in sustainable forests.
The manufacturing process conforms to the environmental
regulations of the country of origin.

For India and Maya,

who always get back

in the saddle

Chapter 1

Sam took a deep breath and held it before peering over the top of the stable door. It was as bad as she thought. Mulberry had managed to make soup out of her bedding overnight. What had been golden shavings smelling of fresh cut wood were now brown and soggy. Sam sighed. It would be a nightmare to clean up. Mulberry munched her hay and watched Sam closely, her black eyes gleaming with mischief.

'You might as well take a breath and start working, two-legs,' she said. 'This mess isn't going to clear itself up.'

Sam pulled a face at her. 'You did this deliberately,' she said.

'Did not!' Mulberry said, a look of mock innocence on her face.

'Then how come the corner of the stable where you sleep is nice and clean?' Sam asked.

Mulberry stopped chewing and looked down her long nose at Sam. 'Well, I'm hardly going to lie in my own poo, am I?' she said. 'Do I look like a pig to you?'

'Comparing you with pigs is insulting to pigs,' Sam said. 'You are much, much worse.'

Mulberry lifted her top lip to bare her teeth in a grin and shook her mane. 'Well, right now, you are like a sheep: bleat, bleat, bleat,' Mulberry said. 'Or perhaps a dog, constantly whining. Either way, it's not getting this stable mucked out and that's what you're here for, so get to it.'

Sam slid back the bolts on the stable door and pushed her wheelbarrow into the opening to block Mulberry in case she decided to make a run for it. Not that there was much chance of that when the greedy little mare still had hay to guzzle down. Sam dug her shavings fork into the flattened poo and groaned as she strained to lever it off the floor.

'What did your last slave die of?' she asked Mulberry.

'Don't give me that,' scoffed the jet-black pony. 'You lot could leave us alone, roaming fields and woods to our hearts' content, skipping around the countryside. But no, you have to stick a saddle on our backs and an iron bit between our teeth and make us do stuff for your pleasure. The least you can do in return is clean up a bit of poo. I don't like being stuck in a stable, you know, it plays havoc with my asthma.'

Sam paused from forking shavings into the wheelbarrow, her jaw dropping in disbelief. 'You don't have asthma!'

Mulberry stuck her nose up in the air. 'I cough from time to time,' she said. 'That's a sure sign that something is going wrong with my lungs.'

'Oh, rubbish,' Sam said, sweat beginning to shine on her forehead with the effort of clearing up Mulberry's mess. 'You make this stuff up to get out of doing any work!'

'I'm telling you, keeping me in this stable is bad for my health,' Mulberry insisted.

'Your health is fine,' Sam said. 'As far as

we know. If you behaved better for the vets, they wouldn't want danger money to go anywhere near you and you might get check-ups more often. Look what you did to the last one!'

'He shouldn't sneak up on people with needles then, should he?' Mulberry grumbled.

'He was trying to give you a vaccination,' Sam said. 'He needed stitches for that bite you gave him!'

'He only needed two or three from what I heard,' Mulberry said.

'Two or three still counts as STITCHES!' Sam said.

'Oh, hush!' Mulberry said, pulling a mouthful of hay from her hay net and pushing it against Sam's lips. 'You're wasting away, have some breakfast.'

'Get off!' Sam said, pushing at Mulberry's chest and giggling.

'Yum, yum,' Mulberry said, rubbing the hay against Sam's face making her shriek with laughter. 'This is good stuff, part of your five a day. Plenty of roughage for nice, healthy droppings.'

They went quiet at the sound of leather-booted footsteps approaching Mulberry's

stable. Mulberry went back to eating and Sam worked faster as a thin, bony figure appeared by the wheelbarrow, blocking some of the sunlight and making the stable gloomy. Sam put down the rake and tried not to gulp with fear as she looked up at the sharp face of Miss Mildew, the owner of both Meadow Vale Riding School and Mulberry.

Miss Mildew narrowed her eyes and pressed her colourless lips together so tightly, they almost disappeared. Her straight black hair was scraped back into a tight bun and she was dressed as neatly as ever in a green tweed riding jacket, cream jodhpurs, black leather boots, and white shirt. Miss Mildew glared into the stable, sweeping her cold blue eyes over Mulberry, looking for something to find fault with. The little black mare pulled a face and laid her ears back against her head.

'I would have thought this stable would be clean by now,' Miss Mildew snapped.

'I'm sorry, Miss Mildew, I'm going as fast as I can,' Sam said. 'Mulberry has been a bit messy this morning . . . '

'It's a poor horsewoman who blames her horse,' Miss Mildew interrupted, while Mulberry threw Sam an angry look over her shoulder. 'When I agreed to let you join the other helpers up here, Miss Grey, I didn't think you would spend all day talking to yourself, while jobs were left undone.'

'No, Miss Mildew,' Sam said. 'Sorry, Miss Mildew.'

'I have a family coming to view Mulberry in an hour and a half,' Miss Mildew said.

'She must be groomed and tacked up, ready to be ridden. I expect her and her saddle and bridle to be immaculate and gleaming.'

'Yes, Miss Mildew,' Sam said, her heart sinking.

'I have high hopes of getting a good price for her, considering how well she performed at the Summer Show,' Miss

Mildew said. A small, smug smile played about her lips as she walked away. There was nothing Miss Mildew loved more than money.

Sam's throat ached at the thought of Mulberry being sold. Yes, Mulberry had been wonderful at the Summer Show; she was a brilliant pony, fast and talented. But she was also bad-tempered and stubborn and until Sam had persuaded Mulberry to let her ride on her back, no one at the riding school had had the nerve to ride her for a long time. They were a partnership but it seemed no one else could see that. Not big sister Amy or even Mum, who wouldn't buy Mulberry because she didn't trust her not to hurt Sam. Mulberry would never do that, Sam knew it. They were perfect for each other and Sam wanted Mulberry to be hers more than anything else in the world. Sam brushed a tear out of her eye as she carried on mucking out. It seemed that by Christmas, another little girl would be grooming Mulberry and riding her in shows. It wasn't fair.

Chapter 2

Sam took her time grooming Mulberry. She had been planning on riding today anyway, so Mulberry's saddle and bridle were clean and polished to a rich shine. As she ran the brush over Mulberry's glossy black sides she noticed it was getting thicker and fluffier as her winter coat grew in. The satin was turning into plush and Sam could grip the hair on Mulberry's ribs between her fingertips. The little mare sighed with contentment as Sam brushed her coat until it gleamed and worked her fingers through Mulberry's shaggy mane until all the knots and tangles were gone.

She knew what Mulberry was going to say but the question was itching on her lips so Sam decided to go ahead and ask it anyway. 'What if I were to buy you, Mulberry?'

'Not this conversation again,' Mulberry said. 'I told you two-legs, it would take too much time to train you up. Besides, I'm not going anywhere unless it's the right home. I might not be going anywhere at all.'

'What do you mean?' Sam asked.

'Nothing,' Mulberry said.

'You'd better not be planning anything silly, Mulberry,' Sam warned.

'The thought never crossed my mind!'

Sam narrowed her eyes at the little mare as she began to gently brush Mulberry's face clean, but she decided not to get into an argument. 'What kind of home do you want then?' she asked.

'I want a child that goes to lots of shows,' Mulberry said. 'I miss being the centre of attention, winning rosettes, getting applause, all that stuff. I want to be out showjumping again, doing cross-country, all the dangerous stuff. And no offence, but your Mum is not going to let you do the dangerous stuff, is she?'

'No, I suppose not,' Sam said in a small voice.

'See, I need someone with loads of confidence who is going to let me have fun every time I'm ridden, without an interfering mother who expects me to babysit all the time,' Mulberry blabbed on, ignoring Sam's unhappiness. 'They have to have lots of fields for me to graze in so I hardly ever have to come into a stable, good food, and lots of green apples. Perfect.'

'Maybe if we proved to Mum there is nothing to worry about . . . ' Sam said.

'I'm not proving anything!' Mulberry snapped. 'I haven't put a foot wrong and she still doesn't trust me. OK, I may have chucked you off a couple of times in the beginning but that was to make you a better rider.'

'Thanks!' Sam said, her voice loaded with sarcasm. 'But Mum doesn't interfere with Amy and Velvet . . . '

'Not interested,' Mulberry said. 'Why should I work so hard to convince someone who is set against me?'

'Let's hope these people are nice then,' Sam said, her heart breaking just a little.

'They need to be more than nice—they need to be perfect!' Mulberry said. 'Make sure you get any shavings out of my tail, it doesn't look very professional, having shavings in your tail.'

Sam rolled her eyes. 'Thanks, but I know how to groom.'

Sam thought about what Mulberry had said. 'Mulberry, you know there is no such thing as perfect, don't you? Never, ever.'

''Course there is,' Mulberry said. 'Horses up here go on about having the perfect rider and the perfect home all the time. Why shouldn't I have just the same?'

'Life isn't perfect for them, Mulberry. They're just happy,' Sam said.

'Rubbish!' Mulberry said. 'Perfect exists and I'm not being sold unless I get it!'

Sam sighed and shook her head. She

loved the fact that she seemed to be the only person at the stables who could talk to the animals and hear them talking back, but sometimes understanding animals was hard. She loved Mulberry to bits but trying to untangle the way she thought gave Sam a headache. If Mulberry thought she was right, there was no arguing with her. This was just an example of Mulberry's twisted logic—she liked living at Meadow Vale stables, she liked Sam. Sam could not understand why Mulberry was so reluctant to be sold to her, or to be sold at all. It didn't make sense—surely Mulberry knew there was no such thing as the perfect home?

But Sam knew arguing was pointless. She decided she would talk to Mulberry about this later—it wasn't as if any buyer could be as perfect as Mulberry wanted.

After Sam had brushed down Mulberry's legs and put oil on her hard little blue hoofs to make them shine, she picked up the saddle and bridle from the tack room, made her way back to the stable, and slipped them onto an unusually obedient Mulberry. So keen was the little mare to meet a possible new owner that she didn't clamp her teeth together and stick her head up in the air as she usually did when Sam tried to slip the bit into her mouth. Instead, she lowered her head, opened her lips and allowed Sam to guide the steel bit over her tongue. Sam gently eased the saddle down Mulberry's back, careful not to ruffle the thickening coat, and fussed with buckles and the little leather keepers that held all the thin straps flat against the bridle. She tweaked the saddlecloth so it lay smooth beneath the girth and was at last satisfied that Mulberry looked perfect.

'What time is it?' Mulberry asked.

Sam looked at her watch. 'Time to go,' she said, as she leaned over the stable's half door and slipped back the bolt from the inside.

'Excellent!' Mulberry squealed and almost knocked Sam flat on her back as she barged her way out of the stable. 'Let's get ready to rrrrrrumble!'

Sam grabbed at the reins as Mulberry rushed past and dug her heels in to slow the pony down.

'That is NOT the attitude Mulberry!' Sam cried, as Mulberry rushed through the cool and calm of the bottom yard and out into the bright sunshine.

Meadow Vale Riding School was busy with pupils being dropped off and picked up for lessons. Liveries, people who paid Miss Mildew to keep their own animals at the yard, were busy feeding and watering their horses. Mulberry pranced through the yard, snorting with pride as she lifted her hoofs high with every step. Sam's mood lightened a bit as she watched people turn and smile with admiration as Mulberry went past. The steel on her tack flashed bright and her coat was a deep, glossy velvet. No matter how bad-tempered Mulberry was, Sam knew that right now everyone on the yard would admit that Mulberry was a beautiful pony.

Except one. Apricot was a little Shetland pony who delighted in teasing Mulberry at every chance she could get. Nothing made

Apricot happier than making Mulberry lose her temper.

'Oooh, look at Miss Fancy Pants!' Apricot jeered. Mickey and Turbo, the other Shetlands who shared a space in the barn with her, sniggered behind her back. 'Think you're something special, don't yer?'

Mulberry stopped and lowered her head towards Apricot, sending a blast of air through her nostrils that blew the little Shetland's forelock back.

'I *am* something special,' Mulberry said, in what Sam thought was a remarkably calm voice—for Mulberry. 'So special, that someone wants to buy me. If you were sold it would probably be for donkey rides on the beach.'

'Oh yeah?' Apricot said. 'Well, they might think you're a bit too long in the tooth to be worth the money Mildew's askin' for yer. Might be, meat money is all they'll be offering for *you*.'

Mickey and Turbo rolled about in the hay, shrieking with laughter, while Basil, the huge cob who lived next door, simply rolled his eyes as he munched on his hay. Mulberry stalked off, her long nose in the air, towing Sam in her wake.

Mulberry said nothing as she walked

past the top yard, past the office, and over to the outdoor arena. Sam prayed Apricot's insults hadn't put Mulberry into too foul a mood. She cringed as Mulberry ground

her teeth on the steel bit, cracking the metal between her square, yellow teeth.

'Let's go and meet these people, shall we?' Sam asked, a little nervously. She saw Miss Mildew and Janey, the head girl, talking to a family beside the arena gate. 'I bet they are really nice. Not perfect, but nice.'

Mulberry just snorted and shook her mane.

Chapter 3

The Dawlishes stood by the arena, waiting for Mulberry. The mother, father, and their three boys all had golden hair and skin tanned to the colour of brown sugar. They were all grinning excitedly, chattering amongst themselves about meeting the pony for the first time. Perhaps Mulberry would let herself be sold today? Sam sneaked a peek at Mulberry from the corner of her eye but the little mare was gazing all around her with a bored expression. If Mulberry was impressed, she was doing a very good job of hiding it. As she led Mulberry to the gate, Sam

could hear what Janey was saying to them.

'I really think it would have been best if your sons had groomed and tacked Mulberry up before riding her,' Janey said, her brow knotted in a frown. 'She's a good mare when you get on the right side of her but she can be prickly and needs firm handling. The boys would be best seeing if that is something they are comfortable with.'

'Oh, really, it's not important,' the mother said, beaming her big white smile and waving a hand in the air. 'If we do decide to buy the mare, our staff will be looking after her. Our boys will not need to handle at her at all. As long as they can ride her, it will be fine.'

'Of course they'll be able to ride her,' Miss Mildew said, her face turning slightly pink as she darted a glance of annoyance at Janey. 'All the ponies and horses I sell have perfect manners and can be ridden by any child or handled by the most nervous beginner. Mulberry is as good a pony as I have ever sold and is very talented. She will take your boys far in Pony Club.'

The Dawlishes smiled at this while

Janey said nothing. Miss Mildew pointed at Sam. 'This girl here is one of my pupils,' she declared. 'She's not my best rider but Mulberry is so forgiving and moves so well, she makes her look wonderful.'

Sam felt her cheeks burn with embarrassment at Miss Mildew's words. The Dawlishes looked uncomfortable, and Janey looked so angry Sam was waiting to see if steam would come out of her ears. She looked at Mulberry, who was glaring all around her but at no one in particular. The last thing she looked was forgiving.

Mr Dawlish cleared his throat. 'Well, we would love to see Mulberry being put through her paces.'

Sam nodded and led Mulberry into the centre of the arena. She quickly slid her hand between the girth and Mulberry's belly to make sure it was snug. Mulberry had a cheeky habit of holding her breath when Sam was doing up her girth—it made it so loose that on one occasion, the saddle had slid around when Sam put her weight into the stirrup to mount up and she had fallen flat on her back. Mulberry had laughed herself sick. Now she always checked before getting on and always wore her body protector.

'They seem nice, Mulberry,' she whispered as she ran her stirrups down and gathered up her reins. 'They have staff—sounds like a good home. They won't run out of food anytime soon.'

'Hmmph,' Mulberry said.

'Be nice!' Sam whispered, as she swung her leg over Mulberry's back. 'Or they might not buy you.'

It took a few seconds for Mulberry to get into the swing of working—Apricot had upset her. But Mulberry loved to be ridden and within a few seconds Sam was helping her show off her smart walk, her lovely bouncy trot, and, finally, her gliding canter, during which she looked every inch the perfect pony, neck arched, mane flowing. Sam kept her breathing even and her hands and body as still as possible— Mulberry hated a rider who fidgeted and fussed in the saddle. Janey was right: Mulberry was prickly. But Sam knew that if she didn't hold the little mare's head too tightly and sat quietly, like she was just watching TV, then the mare would respond to every press of her leg as she asked for walk, trot, and canter. Sam turned her gently into figures of eight and circles so

Mulberry swooped like a swallow around the school.

Sam was loving it as much as Mulberry and her heart broke to hear the 'oohs' and 'aahs' coming from the Dawlishes by the arena wall. *They like her*, she thought, as she asked Mulberry to stop simply by bringing her shoulders back and sitting deep into the saddle. *They will buy her today before I get the chance to talk to her, or Mum, and I will never see her again.*

'Well, that was very impressive,' Mrs Dawlish said, beaming her big smile. 'Your turn, Georgie. Let's see how you get on.' And with that, her eldest son crammed a riding hat on his head, jumped down from the wall (which made Mulberry start in surprise), and walked across the wood chip surface. He put a hand on the reins. 'You can get down now,' he said to Sam. She looked down at his face; a slight sneer played about his lips. Georgie, she decided, wasn't a very nice person. Maybe they were not so perfect after all?

Sam had no choice but to dismount and hand him the reins, while Mulberry sniffed at him with mistrust. She clearly didn't think much of the rude little boy who had startled her. Sam held on to the stirrup to stop the saddle moving on Mulberry's back and hurting her as Georgie pulled himself into the seat. She was glad she did, as she was horrified to see Georgie mount as badly as a beginner on their first lesson. He practically climbed hand over hand to get into the saddle, his weight dragging on Mulberry. He actually pulled the little mare towards him, he was mounting so roughly. Sam swallowed as Mulberry's eyes narrowed with temper.

Once mounted, Georgie's riding didn't get any better. Despite his mother telling Miss Mildew that he was a very talented rider and really needed a pony that would let him win at competitions, he looked very nervous. He leaned forward in the saddle, throwing himself and Mulberry off balance; he held the reins so short poor Mulberry's chin was yanked down against her chest and she could barely see where she was going; when he wanted her to go from walk to trot, he flapped his arms like a chicken and kicked her repeatedly. Sam winced at the sound of his kicks on Mulberry's ribs and she looked at Janey. The instructor's face was white and angry as she watched the boy. Miss

Mildew and Mrs Dawlish were chattering away and Georgie's little brothers shouted encouragement, 'Make her go faster, Georgie, make her gallop!'

The canter was awful. Any experienced rider would know that to ask for canter you sit deep, do not rise to the trot, put your outside leg behind the girth and squeeze, and a well-schooled horse would understand what you are asking for and glide effortlessly into canter. Not Georgie. He kept his tight, hard grip on Mulberry's mouth, leaned forward, kicked her so hard Sam could hear the breath whooshing from her body and yelled, 'CanTOR, canTOR!' in her ear. It was the worst way Sam had ever seen anyone ask for canter.

Mulberry did not react well. She carried on in the fast trot Georgie had forced her into and ignored him when he screamed in her ear. Sam knew that Georgie had to ask her to canter properly in the next five seconds or things were going to get ugly. She looked at Janey to see if she was going to step in but then Mulberry finally lost her temper and did exactly what Georgie's little brothers wanted her to do—she took off, galloping around the arena. Georgie screamed and clung on by wrapping both arms around her neck, reins forgotten and

dangling, before Mulberry did her famous Sliding Stop. She slid to a halt, churning up wood chips, while throwing her body backwards, so fast that Georgie lost his balance and was catapulted, wailing, over her shoulder to land with a resounding thud on the arena floor.

There was a split second of silence as they all stared, open mouthed, and then Georgie started screaming, his brothers started crying, and Mr Dawlish started shouting, 'This is NOT what the advert said I could expect!' Mrs Dawlish ran into the arena shrieking, 'My poor baby!', while Mulberry simply walked into a corner and turned her back, her big bum facing them all. Miss Mildew strode into the arena and pointed her whip at Sam.

'Get that animal out of here!' she barked

before hurrying over to help Mrs Dawlish, who was rocking Georgie like a baby. Georgie, Sam couldn't help but notice, was also crying like one. She ran to Mulberry, grabbed the reins, and hurried her from the arena.

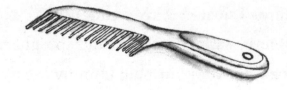

Chapter 4

'Mulberry, that was such a bad thing to do!' Sam said, breathless with fear and little bit of glee, if she was honest. She hurried Mulberry away from the outdoor arena so fast, the little mare had to trot to keep up.

'Did you hear him?' Mulberry demanded, outraged. '"CanTOR, canTOOOOR." Ninny! I would have "canTORed" if he hadn't been holding my head so tight that my knees were hitting me in my face!'

'Oi!' Apricot called. 'Back already?'

'What happened, did they spot your wrinkles?!' Turbo asked.

'Come out here and say that,' Mulberry roared, lunging at the barn gate, ears back, teeth snapping as the Shetlands squealed with laughter and ran to the back of the barn, out of Mulberry's reach.

'You'll have to move faster than that!' Mickey yelled.

'Ignore them!' Sam said as she pulled hard on the reins and dragged a furious Mulberry through the car park, where everyone had stopped what they were doing and was now staring at Mulberry in surprise rather than admiration. Sam trotted Mulberry to the bottom yard, rushed her into her cool stable, and hurried to get her tack off, while the angry little pony scraped at the floor with one hoof and ground her teeth.

'That boy was a fool!' she declared as

Sam eased the bridle over her head.

'Yes, he was,' Sam said in a soothing voice as she struggled to unbuckle Mulberry's girth. Mulberry swung her head round and nipped Sam on the arm.

'Ow!' Sam said, rubbing her arm. 'What was that for?'

'For talking to me like I'm a foal,' Mulberry said. 'Don't try that sing-song tone of voice with me, like I'm being unreasonable. That boy couldn't ride a loose gate on a windy day and you know it!'

A figure loomed in the doorway and Mulberry and Sam looked up to find Janey staring at them. 'Well,' Janey said. 'That was fun, wasn't it?'

'She didn't mean it,' Sam stammered as she slipped Mulberry's saddle from her back.

'Yes, she did, don't be making excuses for her,' Janey said. Mulberry put her ears back but Janey reached out a hand and scratched her on the forehead. Mulberry sighed and relaxed. 'Not that I blame her. "Staff" indeed!' Janey snorted. 'They weren't the right people for our Mulberry. She wants a rider who's going to groom her, handle her, bond with her, and get

to know all her funny little ways, not some spoilt little boy who is only going to ride her in shows to win prizes. Our Mulberry needs someone who cares, don't you little lady?' Mulberry lidded her eyes and practically purred as Janey scratched away. 'She needs someone like you, Sam.'

Sam and Mulberry watched Janey walk away. 'Did you hear that, Mulberry?' Sam asked. 'It looks like I'm the perfect one after all!'

Mulberry snorted and butted Sam affectionately with her shoulder.

'I'm going to try and talk to Mum again,' Sam said.

'No point . . . What was the look on his face like?' Mulberry asked, her eyes gleaming.

Sam widened her eyes until they bulged

from her face, opened her mouth into a wide O, and pulled the corners of her lips down. Mulberry lifted her top lip and brayed like a donkey with laughter, while Sam slid down the stable door, hands clapped over her mouth to stifle her giggles as Mulberry whinnied and said 'CanTOR, canTOR!'

'You're so naughty, Mulberry!'

The little mare lowered her head and brushed Sam's face with her soft lips and nose, blowing a sharp breath through her nostrils that smelt of sweet hay. 'Made you laugh though, didn't I?'

Sam reached up and linked her fingers just behind Mulberry's ears and planted a big kiss on the soft plush of Mulberry's nose. 'So we're still looking for perfect, are we?'

'Still looking,' Mulberry agreed.

Which gives me more time to talk Mum around, Sam thought.

It didn't seem to matter who came to view her, Mulberry didn't like them. She found fault with every rider and tried every trick she knew to get them off. There was the

Sliding Stop that she had tried with the Dawlishes. Then there was the Wall of Death, where she raced round the school, not paying any attention to the crying child on her back, who frantically tugged on the reins. Then there was the Spin and Drop, where she would spin to the side and drop one shoulder at the same time, flinging her rider to the ground. With one little girl (who really had been too young for Mulberry), she simply stood in the middle of the school and refused to move at all. The child flapped the reins and waved a whip in the air as Mulberry dozed off. She had burst into

tears of frustration and ended up being lifted out of the saddle by her mother. One girl had such bad balance in the saddle that all Mulberry had done was shake herself like a dog and she had simply slid off to land with a thump on the floor of the school, reins still clutched firmly in one hand. Sam had to choke back a laugh. She

didn't know who looked more surprised, the rider or Mulberry! 'I didn't even try to get her off,' Mulberry had confessed. 'I was just trying to get rid of a fly that was tickling my ribs.'

The weeks wore on. The weather was getting colder, the nights longer and the number of people wanting to come and view Mulberry, fewer. Sam counted the money she had saved in her bank account and told her mother how wonderful Mulberry was every chance she had. But Mum was hearing the reports of Mulberry's bad behaviour and she pressed her lips into a thin line every time Sam mentioned her name. Miss Mildew's temper was getting shorter as well and she shouted and snapped at Sam every time Mulberry misbehaved for a possible buyer as if it was all Sam's fault. Even Janey was looking worried. 'This is not going to do the stubborn little madam any good,' she said to Sam. 'People don't normally buy ponies in the winter, children don't get a chance to ride much after school with the short evenings. If Mulberry doesn't get settled soon, she might not go before next spring and Miss Mildew won't be happy about that.'

'Is that so bad?' Sam asked. She hoped Mulberry wouldn't go at all and things would stay the same.

'Seeing as Mulberry won't work as a riding school pony, Miss Mildew might just be tempted to give her away to the first person who'll take her,' Janey said. 'And the kind of people who come crawling out of the woodwork when a pony is advertised as free . . . well.'

'Well what?' Sam asked.

Janey frowned, her brown eyes dark with worry. 'You might get nice people coming forward,' she said, nibbling her lower lip. 'Families who have the time and money to keep a pony but not the cash up front to buy them. But she may get some horrible dealers sniffing about, the type of dealer who would work Mulberry so hard before a viewing that she would be too tired to move and sell her on as the perfect first pony for a small child to a family who know nothing about horses. When Mulberry returns to her usual lively self, she'll scare the child and the parents and she'll end up unsellable, because everyone will think she is dangerous.'

Mulberry shuddered and Sam widened her eyes in horror.

'That would never happen to Mulberry!' she said.

'The thing is, a pony doesn't have to be dangerous to get a reputation,' Janey said. 'All it takes is for enough people to *say* it's dangerous. And then no one will take it on. Mulberry was retired from the riding school for being naughty. You made her look good at the Summer Show but now, with all the riders she has thrown in the last couple of weeks, people are beginning to ask questions again. Miss Mildew doesn't like it when people ask questions.' Janey looked down at Sam. 'I know you want to keep Mulberry, but if you want her to be happy, then make her behave.'

'How?' Sam asked.

Janey shook her head, her brown curls rippling. 'I have no idea, but you're just about the only person she listens to. Get her to behave or who knows where she will end up?'

Chapter 5

Sam stared after Janey in horror as the riding instructor walked away. She looked at Mulberry but the little black mare was munching away on her hay net and didn't look in the slightest bit upset at what Janey had just said.

'Did you hear that?' Sam asked.

''Course I did,' Mulberry said. 'She was only standing two feet away from me and I'm not deaf.'

'Aren't you worried?' Sam asked.

'Nope,' Mulberry said. 'I'm quality I am, even if your Mum can't see it. I'm bound to get the perfect home.'

'Mulberry, this isn't funny,' Sam said. 'Perfect homes DO NOT EXIST. I keep telling you this. You have to make your mind up about being sold.'

'I will. When the perfect home comes along,' said Mulberry stubbornly. 'One's bound to come along sooner or later.'

'One did—but I'm still not perfect am I?' Sam said, tears pricking her eyes.

'Don't,' Mulberry said. 'I don't want to talk about you.' And she simply turned her back on Sam.

'Fine, be like that!' Sam yelled, and she stomped away.

Sam's whole body fizzed and popped with anger as she walked through the car park. Dealing with Mulberry was so frustrating, there were times she felt she could load the little mare onto a lorry herself and happily wave goodbye. The fact that Mulberry was now in trouble and wouldn't change her behaviour was enough to make Sam scream.

There was only one person Sam could talk to about this. She passed the barn where the Shetlands were munching their hay. Apricot stared at her with big eyes and a mock-innocent expression, but didn't say anything. Sam marched past and turned into the top yard, where all the big horses, liveries, and riding school animals, were kept.

Sam stomped down the corridor between the stables. The horses all flinched as she passed, sensing her terrible mood. She stopped outside the door of Velvet, her mother's horse, and peered over the top. The mare pulled a face and shook her thick black mane.

'Calm down, little 'un,' she said, in her low, sweet voice. 'You're so angry we can taste it!'

Lucy, Janey's big black and white mare,

popped her head over her stable door, which was next to Velvet's. She narrowed her eyes and flattened her ears against her head. 'I've got a headache already,' she said. 'Whatever is the matter?'

'Mulberry!' Sam said.

Lucy and Velvet looked at each other and rolled their eyes. 'What's the naughty little mare done now?' Velvet asked.

'She keeps throwing anyone who comes to ride her,' Sam said. 'Janey says if this carries on Miss Mildew will give her away. What's wrong with her? It's like she doesn't she want to be sold.'

At the sound of that last word—sold—a ripple seemed to run through the rows of stables. Horses whinnied anxiously and popped their heads over their doors. One small, nervous little chestnut mare began to rock from side to side, a bad habit her owners were trying to stop. Lucy and Velvet shuddered.

'Sold!' Velvet said. 'Every horse hates that word.'

'It would serve Mulberry right,' a big brown gelding declared.

'Don't you say that!' Lucy snapped, baring her huge yellow teeth. 'We don't say that, not about any pony or horse, no matter how bad they've been.'

'But I don't understand,' Sam said. 'Mulberry said she wanted to be sold, she said she wanted to go to a new home.'

'Lies and hot air,' Lucy said. 'Mulberry's full of both.'

'No horse really wants to get sold, little 'un,' Velvet said gently. 'They get loaded up onto that lorry and they don't know what they're travelling to. Kind owners or cruel? A warm stable in winter when you are cold, a rug on your back when it's raining, or no shelter at all? Food in your belly when you are hungry or just weeds to pick at? A vet when you are sick or left to suffer? And for little ponies like Mulberry, there is the fear that the children they are bought for will forget about them and leave them, lonely and sad in the field. Mulberry doesn't want to go to a home like that.'

'But she ain't going to admit it,' Lucy said. 'Not her.'

'So she's stalling,' Velvet said. 'She might not like it here but at least she knows how she's going to be treated.'

'But I love her!' Sam said. 'I wouldn't forget about her or leave her cold and hungry! But she keeps telling me she doesn't want me to talk to Mum about buying her!' Sam began to cry, hot tears spilling down her cheeks.

Velvet and Lucy looked at each other and shook their heads.

'I reckon her heart's broken,' Lucy said. Velvet nodded in agreement.

'What do you mean?' Sam asked.

'When Mulberry was a riding school pony, she'd find a child she'd like,' Lucy said. 'They would have fun together for a year, maybe two, and then the child would outgrow her and move onto something else. Once they stopped riding her, they never talked to her or groomed her again, it was like she didn't exist anymore. She'd wait for them to come up and they would walk past her as if she was invisible or, even worse, they would say something like, "I used to ride her but I ride something much better now," and you'd see her shoulders droop with misery. After a few years, she stopped trying to bond at all.'

'But I wouldn't do that to her,' Sam

sobbed. 'I love her so much!'

'I reckon she knows that, but she doesn't know if she can trust you yet, Sam,' Velvet said. 'Give her time—if your heart had been broken as often as Mulberry's, would you be so quick to put it in someone else's hands again?'

'Oh!' Sam said. 'I had no idea.' She reached up a hand and stroked Velvet's long, soft nose. The big black mare rumbled deep in her throat and dropped her head so that Sam could trace the outline of the white star on her forehead with her fingertips.

'Do you worry about being sold, Velvet?'

The mare crinkled her eyes and shook her head. 'Never,' she said in her sweet, low voice. 'Your mother loves me too much. We've bonded and now we're a

pair. It would be wrong to split us up.'
Sam smiled and kissed Velvet on the nose.

'But I don't think I have much time to convince Mulberry or Mum,' Sam said. 'Janey is saying Miss Mildew might give Mulberry away if she doesn't start to behave and I can't force her to accept me, can I? She has to want to be with me, doesn't she?'

'She does want to be with you, Sam,' Velvet said. 'But Mulberry was on her own for so long before you came along she's frightened she'll be left behind again. She's so scared she can't see the problems she's causing herself by being so stubborn. If anyone can get through to her, it's you.'

Sam sighed, while Lucy laid her long head on top of her stable door and gazed at Sam with big brown eyes and Velvet licked her face with a rough, warm tongue. Sam had to get Mulberry to see sense.

Chapter 6

The next family who came to see Mulberry seemed really nice. They knew what they were doing—the parents both rode and were looking for a pony for their little girl, Poppy, who was having riding lessons and was desperate for a pony of her own. She helped Sam tack Mulberry up and she seemed a little in love with her already.

'She is so beautiful,' Poppy said as she stroked Mulberry's coat with one small hand. 'And she's jet black too, just like Black Beauty.' Over Poppy's head, Mulberry rolled her eyes. Sam gave her a warning look. 'I just know she'll be perfect for me. I so want a pony of my own, I want to brush it and groom it and feed it and be able to ride along with my parents. And we can enter shows and get lots of rosettes!' She looked up at Sam, her blue eyes shining. 'She'd do all that with me,

wouldn't she? I'd love her and she would be really happy.'

Sam swallowed a lump in her throat. 'Mulberry would love a home like that.' She glared at Mulberry. 'Wouldn't you?' Mulberry pulled a face but said nothing.

'You're funny,' Poppy giggled. 'You talk like she understands every word you are saying.'

'Well, I think ponies do understand what we are saying,' Sam said. 'I just don't think we notice them listening.'

Poppy nodded, her reddish curls bouncing. 'I think that too,' she whispered.

After all the disasters that had happened so far with the viewings, Janey had insisted that Poppy ride Mulberry in the indoor school for a little while, where the sand surface gave a nice, soft landing, to see how they got on. The only problem was, Poppy's younger brother, who Sam suspected was a little jealous that his sister was getting a pony, had insisted on riding too. So Apricot was brought down to the arena for him to ride at the same time Poppy was trying out Mulberry. Sam was worried. She really didn't like the thought of Mulberry and Apricot being so close together, but how was she supposed to stop it? Explain to Miss Mildew that all the ponies did was insult each other until they got into a fight? She was never going to believe that!

Sam walked Mulberry to the indoor school while Poppy ran off to talk to her parents, who were standing on the viewing platform, sipping cups of tea and chatting with Miss Mildew. Janey was already waiting with Apricot when Sam and Mulberry walked in and she held the reins out to Sam. 'Mind the little 'un while I go talk to these people,' she said. 'That girl is tiny and the last thing I want is Miss Mildew telling these people that not only is Mulberry a saint who will never put a hoof wrong, but she will tuck that child into bed every night and read her a story too.'

Sam tried to think of a good reason why she couldn't hold Mulberry and Apricot at the same time but she wasn't quick enough. Before she could open her mouth, Janey had pushed Apricot's reins into her free hand and marched off to join the others. With a sinking heart, Sam stood between the two ponies, who eyed each other with dislike.

'They look like a nice family,' Apricot said, with a sly glance out of the corner of her eye at Mulberry. 'That means they definitely ain't buying you.'

Mulberry snorted. 'Like anyone would be standing in line to buy *you*,' she said. 'A sad sack like yourself, only good for dog treats.'

'Would the two of you please be nice, just for the next hour or so,' whispered Sam. She watched as Poppy skipped towards them, her face lit up with excitement.

'Fart-breath,' Apricot jeered.

'Hippo-face,' Mulberry snapped.

'Washed-up, good-for-nothing, unsellable loser,' Apricot said.

Mulberry moved as fast as a striking snake, but to Sam, it all seemed to happen in slow motion. Mulberry whipped her head round, teeth bared, and lunged at Apricot, who squealed, did a little half rear and spun out of reach. What Mulberry didn't see was Poppy, reaching up to pet her on the nose. Mulberry collided with the child and knocked her flat on the ground. Time seemed to stand still as Mulberry, Sam, and Apricot stared down at Poppy, their jaws hanging open in shock. Poppy stared back at them, her blue eyes glazed with shock and then, to her horror, Sam saw bright red blood pour from Poppy's nose and begin to drip down her chin.

Janey ran over and grabbed Apricot's reins from Sam. Poppy's little brother began to wail, and her parents ran over to Poppy and picked her up, while Miss Mildew simply stood staring at Mulberry. Miss Mildew's face was white with rage and she was gripping her riding whip, twisting it tightly in her hands.

'Get her out of here!' Janey said to Sam.

'It was an accident!' Sam said, tears welling up in her own eyes. 'She didn't see her.'

'I don't care,' Janey said. 'Take her away and keep her out of sight.'

Sam didn't need to be told twice. She ran from the arena with Mulberry, the mare practically cantering as they headed back to her stable.

Chapter 7

The sky had clouded over while they were in the indoor school and cold drops of rain were beginning to splatter down as they ran for Mulberry's stable.

'What have you done?' cried Sam, tears falling down her cheeks.

'I didn't mean it,' Mulberry said, backing into a corner, shaking with fear. 'I didn't! It was an accident; you said it yourself. It's all Apricot's fault!'

'No, it's not, it's yours!' Sam said. 'Why couldn't you ignore her? Why do you always have to start a fight?'

'You heard what she said!' Mulberry

squealed. 'You don't expect me to take that from the likes of her, do you?'

'Oh, Mulberry,' Sam said. 'Sometimes you can be so stupid!'

'What's Mildew going to do?' Mulberry whispered, her voice trembling with fear.

'I don't know,' Sam said, clenching her fingers into fists to stop her hands from shaking. 'I really don't know.'

'Well, she's really done it this time,' said a voice behind them. Sam turned to see Janey staring in at them, her eyes cold and hard as she looked at Mulberry, who flattened her ears and ducked her head in misery. Sam had never seen Janey look at Mulberry like that before. Janey had always loved Mulberry.

'It was an accident,' Sam whispered.

'It doesn't matter,' Janey said. 'A child's

parents just saw what looked like Mulberry attacking their little girl and now the child is injured. After the way she's been behaving the last few weeks, no one is going to touch her with a bargepole now.'

'How is Poppy?' Sam asked.

Janey shrugged. 'She's got a nosebleed and she's had a bad fright. Apart from that, there's not much else wrong with her. It looks like Mulberry must have hit her on the bridge of her nose with her teeth; she's going to have some lovely bruises tomorrow,' Janey looked at Mulberry. 'But she was lucky.'

'What is Miss Mildew going to do to Mulberry?' Sam asked. Mulberry was still staring at the ground and trembling.

'That is up to her,' Jancy said. 'Untack Mulberry and put her out in the field while

Miss Mildew decides.'

'It's raining, can't she stay in her stable?' Sam asked.

'No, Sam,' Janey snapped, her anger beginning to show. 'Get her as far away from everyone as possible. I don't think there is anyone on this yard who wants to be reminded that pony even exists at the moment.'

Sam began to cry again as Janey walked away. Her tears came down as thick and fast as the rain outside as her fingers fumbled with the buckles of Mulberry's tack. The little mare said nothing as Sam slipped a head collar over her face and led her out into the worsening weather. Mulberry plodded along beside her and they both kept their heads down, avoiding looking at anyone as they made their way through a silent yard. Everyone, horse and human, stopped what they were doing to watch them pass. No one said a word, until they began to walk past the Shetland barn.

Apricot was back in the barn with Mickey and Turbo. Mickey began to strike the metal bars of the barn gate with one hoof, slow steady beats that tolled through the yard like a church bell, while Turbo called, 'Going on holiday, Mulberry?', until Apricot shushed them both, watching Mulberry and Sam walk past with dark, sad eyes. The big cobs in the barn next door and all the horses on the top yard walked to their doors, their faces solemn as Sam and Mulberry walked by slowly and began to climb the little hill that led to the fields behind the yard.

No one else was being left out for the

night, so Mulberry was going to be in the field all on her own. The rain was coming down in hard, cold rods now and it mingled with Sam's tears and ran into the corners of her mouth. It sheeted off Mulberry's thick coat and drenched her mane, which clung to her neck like seaweed. Sam threw her skinny arms around Mulberry's neck and sobbed, her face pressed into her mane. Mulberry leaned into her and closed her eyes.

'What are we going to do Mulberry?' Sam wailed. 'What are we going to do?'

Chapter 8

Sam's eyes were hot and itchy from crying all night and her face felt swollen and lumpy. She leaned her cheek against one of the cold stone walls of the top yard and sighed. She had tried to persuade Mum to let her buy Mulberry with the money she had in her savings account. There must be at least £100 in it. All she needed was her mother's signature to get the money out. But Mum had shaken her head.

'I did say we would buy you a pony one day, but the pony has to be the right one for you,' Mum said. 'I just don't think that's Mulberry.'

'But we did so well at the Summer Show,
she doesn't go as well for anyone else, you
know we have a bond . . . ' Sam said.

'Yes, you did ride her well at the Summer
Show,' Mum had interrupted. 'But as for
having a bond, I'm sorry, Sam, I'm not
convinced. I don't think Mulberry is the
type of pony who bonds with anyone. She's

too unpredictable and riding is dangerous enough without having a pony who is bad tempered and vicious.'

'But she's not vicious,' Sam said. 'What happened yesterday was an accident!'

'Sam, I'm sorry, but my mind is made up,' Mum said. 'I'm not wasting my money paying livery on a difficult and possibly dangerous pony. At best, she will destroy your confidence; at worst, she could hurt you very badly.' Mum shook her head again. 'There are lots of good ponies out there looking for a home. When the time is right, we will get one that's perfect for you.'

It didn't matter what Sam said, Mum refused to talk about it anymore. Big sister Amy had looked at Sam with sympathy but she hadn't said anything to back Sam up so she knew she agreed with Mum. So Sam had turned to Velvet.

'Everyone keeps talking about being perfect, but there's perfect on paper and there's perfect in real life. She's not perfect, Velvet, but she is the perfect pony for me,' Sam said as the big black mare stretched her head over the stable door to listen to her. Lucy's ears flicked forward to eavesdrop from the stable next door. 'Mum and Amy are always talking about how riding is a partnership, well, we're partners, me and Mulberry. That's what counts isn't it? There has to be something we can do.'

'Mulberry has gone too far this time,' Velvet said. 'No one trusts her anymore, me included. I wouldn't be happy about you sitting on her back.'

'But . . . ' Sam said.

'There's no "but" about it,' Velvet said. 'She can't be trusted with a young 'un and certainly not one of my young 'uns.'

'She's bitten The Hand That Feeds,' Lucy said. 'There's no going back from that for any animal. There's nothing anyone can do, even if we wanted to. You listen to your mother and to Velvet, Sam. Mulberry is not your problem to solve.'

It didn't matter what Sam said, the two mares didn't want to listen. When she kept trying to argue for Mulberry, they simply turned their bums towards her and dozed off.

Sam needed to try something different. She needed help from someone who was not only clever but a little bit cunning, totally devious, and happy to break the rules or start a fight just for the sake of it.

Sam arrived at the Shetlands' barn a few minutes later. Apricot gazed at her, hay poking out of each side of her mouth as she chewed it slowly and carefully, her eyes lidded. Sam took a deep breath and walked over.

'I need your help,' she said.

'What, no "good morning"?' Apricot asked. 'No, "How are you today, Apricot? You is looking particularly fabulous this fine morning."?'

'You want me to say all that?' Sam asked.

Apricot rolled her eyes. 'It's a bit late now, isn't it? I mean, if you were going to flatter me to appeal to my better nature, then you should have said all that stuff on your own to have a hope of making it sound like you meant it.'

'Honestly Apricot, I haven't a clue what you are on about,' said Sam. Her head was beginning to hurt trying to follow Apricot's logic. 'I wanted to talk to you about Mulberry.'

Apricot made a very rude noise. 'Mulberry, Mulberry, Mulberry. It's always about her!'

'Well, it is at the moment,' Sam said. 'She's the one stuck out in the field all on her own.'

'Yes, and we all know why,' chubby little Turbo said. 'She bit The Hand That Feeds.'

'She did worse than that,' Basil said, in his honey-rich voice. 'She attacked a two-legs foal.'

Mickey shuddered. 'That's as bad as it gets, that is. The two-legs never forgive a pony that hurts one of their foals.'

Basil shook his head. 'I'm going to tell you now, little two-legs, what everyone else has been telling you all morning—there's no helping Mulberry. She'll be given away now and nobody will be asking too many questions about where she goes.'

'It's not right!' Apricot snapped. 'Mulberry deserves better than that. Now,

me and Mulberry, we ain't always seen eye
to eye, but that doesn't mean to say I get
any joy out of seeing her caught out. We
all likes a little nibble from time to time—
keeps the two-legs on their toes.' Apricot
shook her head sadly. 'But Mulberry has
crossed the line—even Janey's set against
her and there ain't that many animals

Janey doesn't like. I don't think there is anything we can do for the old mare.'

Sam crouched down until her eyes were level with Apricot's and gave her a hard stare. 'Well, there had better be something we can do. You're a clever pony, Apricot, and I know you will find a way to help Mulberry. After all, it's your fault she's in this mess in the first place.'

'WHAT?' exclaimed the Shetlands and Basil. Apricot coughed and shuffled her hoofs nervously.

'You and me, we know that Mulberry didn't attack that little girl at all,' said Sam. 'She was going for you, because you were winding her up.'

'Apricot, please tell me you didn't do that,' Basil said, in a stern voice.

'OK, I didn't,' Apricot said.

'Apricot!' Sam snapped.

'OK, OK!' Apricot said. She ducked her head, refusing to look at Turbo and Mickey, and traced a circle in the straw of the barn with one front hoof. 'We had words, you know, like we always do . . . '

'Except you started it,' Sam said.

'That's bad, Apricot, really bad,' Mickey said, in a shocked voice. 'I don't like Mulberry either but you've really landed her in the muck heap.'

''Spose,' Apricot said, in a teeny tiny voice.

'There's no "suppose" about it,' Basil said.

'The question is, what are you going to do about it?' Sam asked.

'I'm thinkin', I'm thinkin',' Apricot said crossly. She was silent for a moment and then she looked up at Sam, her eyes brightening with hope.

'Minnie might know a way,' Apricot said. 'She's been around for years. She knows two-legs, foals and grown-ups, and their ways better'n anyone else on this yard. If anyone can think of an answer, it's Minnie the Moocher.'

Turbo nodded his head, his face thoughtful. 'That she might.'

Basil snorted down his long nose. 'Minnie will be as stumped as the rest of us. Don't be giving the little two-legs hope where there isn't any.'

Apricot cocked her head in Basil's direction. 'Are you standin' too close to that fence? Are ya?'

'What, this fence?' Basil asked, his face a picture of innocence as he sidled closer.

Sam groaned. If anyone stood near what Apricot thought of as her fence, she went bonkers. Calming her down could take all afternoon. Sam clapped her hands inches from Apricot's nose to get her attention.

'Can you focus, please?' Sam said.

Apricot glared at Basil while she talked to Sam. 'What time is it?'

'Lunchtime,' Sam said. 'Why?'

'It means no one's about!' Turbo said gleefully as he began to wriggle under the gate. Sam stared in disbelief as he inched his fat, round body between the bottom bar and the ground and pulled himself free with a pop. Mickey followed soon after and eventually so did Apricot, backing away from Basil and whispering what Sam was sure were dire threats about the consequences of going anywhere near the fence.

'Follow us,' Turbo called over his shoulder as he began to trot through the yard.

'You're going to need us,' Mickey said.

'Minnie is really, really old and she doesn't have much time for two-legs. She might not talk to you if you go to her on your own.'

'Never mind that!' Sam said. 'Are you telling me you lot can let yourselves out of the barn whenever you feel like it? Why hasn't anyone spotted you doing this?'

'We always wait until no one is around.

And Mildew is too cheap to switch on the CCTV cameras,' Apricot said. 'If anyone finds us wandering around, they always think someone forgot to shut the gate properly.'

Sam shook her head and jogged along with the little Shetlands as they trotted through the yard and past the indoor school. She hoped Minnie the Moocher was as clever as they said. She was probably Mulberry's last hope.

Chapter 9

Minnie the Moocher was a very, very old Shetland. She had been one of the first ponies to ever work at Meadow Vale Riding School. She had spent years teaching small children to ride, trekking through the countryside with tiny tots clinging to her back and being led at birthday parties. No one knew how old she was but it was thought she had worked at Meadow Vale for 20 years before she had retired. Now, she spent her days wandering the yard, stealing any feed that people were foolish enough to leave within reach. It was how she got her nickname, Minnie the

Moocher. Although how she ate that feed was a mystery as she had hardly a tooth left in her head.

As Sam and the Shetlands came jogging around the back of the indoor school they found Minnie simply standing by the boundary wall of the yard, soaking up a little bit of the weak sunshine. Her wrinkled eyes were closed, a stiff breeze ruffled her grizzled coat and she didn't move or make any sign that she had heard them.

'Oi!' Apricot said. 'We need to pick your brains about summat.'

Still Minnie ignored them. Turbo bumped Apricot with his shoulder. 'You can't talk to her like that.'

'Why not?' Apricot asked.

'She's old, isn't she?' Mickey said. 'The oldest one up at Meadow Vale Stables.'

'And?' Apricot asked.

'So you have to show her a bit of respect,' Turbo said. 'You know what the oldies are like.'

'You know so much about it, you do it,' Apricot said.

Turbo stretched out his front legs and bent low until his nose touched his knees and his fat belly squished against the ground. 'Oh, old and wise Minnie,' he said in a deep, dramatic voice. Apricot and

Mickey rolled their eyes. 'We come to seek
your advice, we humbly beg that you listen
to our humble pleas, made so humbly . . . '

'Oh, give it a rest,' Minnie said, her eyes
snapping open. She turned to face them,
ears pinned back against her head and her
expression as sour as a lemon. 'You young
ponies have no respect, none at all. I don't
come around bothering you, do I?'

'Only when you're hungry,' Apricot
muttered.

'What did you say?' Minnie snapped.

'Please, we really need your help,' Sam said. 'One of our friends is in big trouble.'

Minnie looked Sam up and down. 'A two-legs that actually listens to ponies,' she snorted. 'I really have seen it all now. I can die happy.' She closed her eyes again. They all stared at her and waited as the seconds ticked by. Sam cleared her throat. 'Um, you're not actually dying right now, are you?'

Minnie's eyes flew open. 'Of course I'm not!' she growled. 'What I was doing was trying to enjoy a bit of sun in peace. Obviously too much to ask for around here.'

'We just need an answer to a question,' Sam said. 'Then we'll leave you alone.'

Minnie sighed. 'Go on then, what is it?'

'A friend of ours, another pony, is in big trouble and we need to get her out of it,' Sam said.

'What did she do?' Minnie asked.

'She got into a fight and knocked over a two-legs foal, but it was an accident,' Sam said.

Minnie sucked her breath in and tutted. 'Nothing worse than hurting a two-legs foal,' she said.

'We know that. We're trying to find a way to get everyone to forgive her,' Sam said.

'Waste of time,' Minnie said. 'Two-legs won't forgive any animal that hurts one of their foals.'

'But there has to be something we can do!' Sam said.

'The only thing you can do is to get the

adult two-legs to change their minds about her,' Minnie said. 'I've watched adult two-legs all my life and they are as different from their foals as two-legs are to ponies. They watch their foals for years, long after they are walking about and eating all by themselves. They cannot bear them to get hurt and it doesn't matter if it's an accident or not, a pony that hurts a two-leg foal is in big trouble. They overreact to everything when it comes to their foals. But a pony who is very kind to a two-leg foal becomes extra special to a two-leg adult. That pony will be forgiven anything if the adults think it will take care of a two-leg foal. Stupid thinking that, but I gave up trying to figure two-legs out a long time ago. But that's your answer— the pony that's good to a two-leg foal is bulletproof.' She thought about that for a second. 'That's just a figure of speech, by the way. I wouldn't try and test that theory with a real bullet.'

An idea was beginning to form in Sam's head. 'So what you are saying is, that if we want to save our friend, we have to get her to do something so all the grown-ups stop seeing her as a devil and see her as an angel instead?' she asked.

'Exactly!' Minnie said.

'Good luck with that,' Apricot said.

'No, I think I have an idea,' Sam said, thinking hard. A smile broke out on her face for the first time in two days. 'But I haven't got much time if it's going to work.' She turned and ran back through the yard, the Shetlands scampering after her like puppies.

'Wheee, we're going to save Mulberry!'
squealed Turbo as his tiny little legs blurred
to keep up with Sam.

'Fantastic,' Apricot said, her voice heavy
with sarcasm, as she ran along beside him.

Minnie watched them go and grumbled to herself. 'That's it, you just run off without so much as a thank you. What else am I standing here all day for but to be of use to you lot? Not like I'm busy is it? My day is packed, I'll have you know, packed . . . ' Her muttering got slower and quieter as she dozed off again.

Chapter 10

It had taken ages for Sam to persuade Miss Mildew to let her ride Mulberry one last time. She had glared at Sam from behind the desk in her office, making Sam's legs shake with nerves.

'That pony is a menace,' Miss Mildew said. 'I really don't think it would be wise to let anyone ride her again. You don't ride quite as well as your sister, so I really don't know how I could face your mother if anything happened.'

'Please Miss Mildew,' Sam said. 'Mulberry has always been good with me; I haven't ever had a problem with her. I love her to bits and it might be the last time I get to ride her.'

'It *will* be the last time you ride her, I am afraid,' Miss Mildew said. 'I'm not a charity, spending my money feeding and sheltering a mare who refuses to work. I don't even like Mulberry.'

'But you do it for Minnie,' Sam said, confused.

'Minnie worked for years at this riding school and never once refused to do her job,' Miss Mildew snapped. 'The least she deserves is a long retirement. Mulberry, however, refuses to cooperate and everyone has to pull their weight at Meadow Vale.'

'Yes, Miss Mildew,' Sam said. 'I do work hard, Miss Mildew . . . '

'I wasn't actually talking about you, Miss Grey, but that pony you seem so fond of,' Miss Mildew said. 'But I am afraid that hanging about her stable all day long, prattling to her and combing out her mane will not make Mulberry like you. You must

put such silly, romantic ideas from your head if you intend to be a rider. Horses must have respect for us and that is all; it is not necessary for them to like us. Get too soft with them and they will walk all over you.'

She glared at Sam. 'I suspect that is the heart of the problem we have with Mulberry. She was never an easy animal in the first place and you spoiling her and treating her like a pet dog has led to her becoming even more badly behaved.' She shook her head. 'I blame myself. I should have parted the pair of you a long time ago.'

'I'm sorry if I have been too soft with Mulberry, but please, please, just let me ride her one last time.' Sam said.

'You seem to be the only one who likes

her,' Miss Mildew sighed. 'Very well then, you can ride Mulberry this afternoon but not alone. If you are going to go for a hack then I want you to take someone with you, just to be on the safe side.'

'May Natalie come with me, Miss Mildew?' Natalie was in the same riding group as Sam at Meadow Vale. She wasn't a very confident rider, but Natalie was the best friend Sam had at Meadow Vale Stables. Sam knew that Natalie would never deliberately make Mulberry sound bad to an adult.

Miss Mildew raised an eyebrow. 'An unusual choice for a hacking partner, Natalie being so terribly nervous,' she said. Miss Mildew sighed and waved Sam away. 'Very well. Run along, Miss Grey. Have your last ride with Mulberry.'

Sam's legs felt rubbery with relief as she ran to the tack room to find a head collar and a lead rope. She headed up to the fields and her heart twisted in her chest to see Mulberry so sad. The little black mare was not even grazing; she simply stood staring dully at the ground, looking lost and lonely in the field all by herself.

'Come on Mulberry, we're going for a ride,' Sam said as she walked over to the pony.

'Go away,' Mulberry said. 'Leave me alone.'

Sam stroked her neck gently. 'You can't just give up.'

'Yes, I can,' Mulberry said. 'Mildew's always had it in for me. She must be so happy now she's got the chance to get rid of me. There's nothing I can do about it.

There's no point fighting for a rider of my own anymore. I'm going to please myself and do absolutely nothing.'

'Don't be silly, you can't give up now,' Sam said. She tried to slip the head collar over Mulberry's head but the mare simply stuck her nose up in the air and put her head out of Sam's reach.

'It's my life, if I want to wallow in self-pity, I shall,' the mare said.

'Well, I've got a plan that might just give you everything you want,' Sam said.

Mulberry rolled her eyes so she could look down at Sam yet still keep her nose

poking skywards. 'Why does that sentence not fill me with joy?' she asked.

'You know, my Dad says sarcasm is the lowest form of wit,' Sam said, planting her hands on her hips and looking sternly at Mulberry.

'Clearly your dad doesn't get out much,' Mulberry said. 'I could show him much lower forms of wit than that.'

'Look, at least drop your head and let me whisper the plan in your ear,' Sam said. 'If you don't like it, I'll go away and leave you alone.'

'Why do you need to whisper it?' Mulberry asked. 'We're the only ones out here. Are you worried about the crows telling tales on you?'

'Trust me, this plan is going to work,' Sam said, grinning. 'I'm not taking any chances that this could go wrong. Those crows can't keep a secret.'

So Mulberry bent her head down and listened while Sam poured the plan into

her ear and the crows wheeled overhead
and complained that they couldn't hear
what she was saying.

Chapter 11

Sam was so nervous the reins felt slippery in her clammy hands. Her body protector felt hot and stiff. She wished she could flick open the Velcro straps that kept it in place and let it fall down to the ground but she knew it was going to come in handy, very, very soon. Sam felt a little sick and she closed her eyes for a moment, listening to Natalie chattering happily alongside her.

'It's so nice to be able to leave the yard and get out of that school!' Natalie said. 'Don't you get bored riding round and round in endless circles? This is the kind

121

of riding I always wanted to do; it's a lot
like the trail riding we do back home.'

'Natalie, you're from New York,' Sam

giggled. 'How much trail riding is there in Central Park?'

Natalie blushed and then giggled too. 'OK, well, not so much where I'm from, but still, it is a great American tradition. Miss Mildew doesn't give us the chance to do it much. And people don't often invite me out with them.'

Sam smiled at Natalie and felt a twist of guilt in her stomach. 'I suppose everyone has their own friends for hacking out with and they don't really think to ask the rest of us,' she said. 'It doesn't help that we're the youngest on the yard.'

'That's OK, you don't have to be nice about it, I know why no one ever asks me to ride along with them,' Natalie said. 'I know it's because I'm nervous and I never want to canter, or jump, or go very fast at all, or go too far from home.'

'Oh, I don't mind about the jumping and stuff,' Sam said. 'But it would be nice to have a little canter though, wouldn't it?' *Please say yes, Natalie, please say yes. We've got to canter for this plan to work!*

But Natalie's face clouded over at the word 'canter'. 'I don't know . . . ' she said, biting her lip and looking down at the pony she was riding.

'Oscar is lovely to canter,' Sam said. 'He never goes very fast. I think he could do with the exercise as well.'

Oscar shot a look of pure annoyance at Sam but it was true; he was quite a round, chubby little pony and it wouldn't hurt him to lose a bit of weight.

'I just get so nervous cantering outside the school,' Natalie confessed. 'It feels so safe inside the school, you know? There is nothing to scare the ponies and, if anything, it's a bit boring for them so they don't get excited. It frightens me that they get so strong and really pull on your arms to go fast when they are outside.'

'I know,' Sam said, trying to keep the worry out of her voice. 'But look, Mulberry is being nice and quiet so you can always tuck Oscar in behind her bum and she will slow him down. As long as we don't let them run neck to neck they won't try and race each other.' Natalie still looked scared. 'Remember what Janey always says if you are nervous about cantering? Get behind the horse in front and let them see nothing but their big bottom. It's only when they see a wide-open space that they get really excited.'

'I guess,' Natalie said. 'Mulberry is being really good today, isn't she? But everyone on the yard has been talking about how horrible she has been lately. I think I'd have been too scared to get on her.'

Sam reached down and patted Mulberry's neck, her thick winter coat dark with sweat from the heat of the afternoon sun. 'Mulberry has always been good for me. There are some woods up ahead and it will be nice and cool to canter under the trees. Why don't we trot until we get to them and you can see how you feel?'

Before Natalie could say anything, Sam pressed her heels against Mulberry's sides to ask her to trot. The little mare responded instantly and behind her Sam heard Natalie yelp with fear as Oscar began to trot too, rushing to catch up with

Mulberry. Sam's guilt felt like a big stone stuck in her throat. She swallowed hard to try and force it back down to her stomach. Sam liked Natalie and she knew she was about to scare her, but she had no choice if her plan was to work. They had to stay together. Sam made a silent promise to do something nice for Natalie when this was all over.

Nerves made Natalie a bad rider. She was doing everything wrong, leaning forward, dropping her toes down so her feet slid right through the stirrup irons, hanging on to Oscar's mouth with short, tight reins. Oscar looked uncomfortable as she bumped along on his back and she looked at Sam with a white face. 'I really don't think I want to canter.'

'It'll be fine,' Sam said. 'You're doing

great! We'll just canter for a few strides and let them have a little fun.'

Natalie was shaking her head, even as Sam sat deep in the saddle, put one leg behind the girth and squeezed with her legs. Mulberry moved smoothly into canter, behaving like the perfect pony that Miss Mildew had advertised and Sam felt like the worst person in the world when she heard Natalie give a short, sharp scream as Oscar cantered after them.

'Sam, stop, please, I think I'm going to fall off!' Natalie yelled.

'Just lean back and sit deep,' Sam called over her shoulder, the wind rushing past her ears. 'Just a few strides and we'll go back to trot.'

As they entered the little woods, where the ground was soft and cool having been protected from the sun's rays by the canopy of leaves overhead, Sam took a deep breath, leaned forward and deliberately flipped herself over Mulberry's shoulder, tucking and rolling as she fell, the way Mulberry had told her to. Sam made sure she came to rest on her tummy, her face hidden by the turf and by her outstretched arms.

Natalie screamed again when she saw Sam fall, and Oscar skidded to a halt next to Mulberry, who had stopped as soon as she felt Sam throw herself from the saddle. Sam could hear Natalie sobbing as she dismounted and ran over to her.

'I knew we shouldn't have cantered, I knew it, I knew it, I knew it,' she sobbed. Sam felt Natalie shake her ever so gently. 'Are you OK, Sam? Are you awake? Please say something.'

When Sam didn't move or say anything Natalie started crying again. 'I told my mom I needed a cell phone. You read about stuff like this happening all the time and with my luck it was bound to happen to me sooner or later. OK, OK, calm down.' Sam heard Natalie take big, deep breaths. She stopped talking to herself for a minute before bursting into tears again.

Sam couldn't stand to hear Natalie crying any more. She sat up and offered her a weak smile, while behind her Mulberry huffed in disgust at Sam changing the plan.

Natalie squeaked with surprise. 'Sam! Are you hurt?'

'Um, no. I kind of fell off deliberately.'

'You did WHAT?' Natalie yelled. She smacked Sam on the arm. 'You scared me half to death!'

'Ow!' Sam clutched at her arm, more in surprise that Natalie, who was normally so shy, had become angry enough to hit her.

'*And* you made me canter!' Natalie said. 'What did you think you were doing?'

'If I don't do something, Miss Mildew is going to sell Mulberry and I will never see her again,' Sam said.

'I don't see how having an accident is going to help,' Natalie said.

'Because it gives Mulberry a chance to prove how much she loves me, seeing as all the adults can't see the obvious. She's going to stay by me and refuse to leave my side.'

Both Natalie and Oscar stared in surprise at Mulberry, who stared back with a '*yeah, and*?' expression on her face.

'How are you going to make her do that?'
Natalie asked.

'Trust me, she will,' Sam said. 'She's not
going anywhere right now, is she? But I
need you to go back to the yard and tell
them I have fallen off and Mulberry is
staying by my side while you get help.'
Natalie frowned. 'Please Natalie, I'd do it
for you,' Sam begged.

'I don't like lying,' Natalie said.

'But you won't be lying,' Sam said. 'I
have fallen off and Mulberry *is* staying
with me.'

Natalie sighed. 'I must be mad,' she
muttered. 'Fine, I'll go back to the yard
and tell them you've had a fall. But that is
all I'm saying.'

Sam grinned at her. 'Thank you, Natalie!
I'll do the same for you one day.'

'No, you won't,' Natalie said, as she swung her leg over Oscar's back. 'I'm not as nutty as you! Are you going to pretend you are unconscious?'

Sam blushed. 'Probably. It looks better that way.'

Natalie shook her head. 'I'm not lying about that; head injuries are serious. I'll say you fainted, if you faint.'

'Huh?' Sam said, and then it dawned on her what Natalie wanted her to do. 'Oh, right.' Sam put her hand to her forehead and swooned to the ground in what she hoped was a convincing way.

'Right, now I'm not lying,' Natalie said, as Oscar began to walk away. 'Faint for as long as you like, I'll be back soon. Don't move—you might have hurt yourself slipping off.'

Chapter 12

After Natalie and Oscar had ridden off in the direction of Meadow Vale Stables, Sam stretched her aching muscles and moved to get up. But she felt Mulberry plant a hoof between her shoulder blades and slam her back down on the ground.

'Mulberry, what do you think you're doing?!' Sam yelled, as she spat turf out of her mouth.

'You've got to keep still and lie in the exact position that what's-her-face, Natalie, left you in, otherwise they'll twig we're lying,' Mulberry said.

'This whole plan isn't going to work unless you look like a hero and it's very hard to look like a hero when I have hoof marks on my back!' Sam said. She slapped at Mulberry's legs. 'Now get off me!'

'Good point,' Mulberry said, backing off. 'I hadn't thought of that.'

Sam sat up and rubbed her shoulder. 'I am going to be so sore tomorrow.'

'Did you relax?' asked Mulberry. 'I told you to try and relax as you fell. When you tense the muscles, that's when they get all bruised from an impact. If you had relaxed when you fell, you wouldn't be hurting now.'

'Mulberry, you try and relax while falling from a cantering pony. It's really not as easy as it sounds. If you want to find out for yourself I can push you out of

the trailer next time we travel somewhere,'
Sam rubbed at her aching neck. 'Do you
know what to do?'

'Yep. As soon as the rescue party turns
up I have to be all heroic.' Mulberry struck
a pose, chest out and neck arched.

'No, Mulberry, this is not about you being
heroic, it's about you being so bonded to
me that you cannot bear to leave my side
when I have an accident, remember?' Sam
said.

'Oh, yeah,' Mulberry said, shoulders
drooping. 'Do we have to? I really don't
want to look like an idiot. I have a
reputation to think of.'

Sam shook her head in disbelief. 'Your
reputation is why we are in this mess in
the first place,' she said. 'If you had just
behaved and been nice to one of those

families that came to see you, you might have been in your new home by now.'

Mulberry sighed. 'I don't want a new home. I can't be bothered with getting to know new people and their ways. Meadow Vale suits me fine.' She nudged at Sam with her soft nose. 'You suit me fine.'

'Oh, Mulberry,' said Sam, her throat closing with tears to hear the little mare finally admit she wanted to be Sam's pony. 'We are supposed to be together. This is going to work, I know it is.'

Mulberry was silent for a moment. It was cool under the trees and Sam could hear a blackbird singing, silvery notes tumbling through the air. She closed her eyes for a moment to enjoy the peace. She really wasn't looking forward to lying to her mother. She heard Mulberry mumble something.

'What did you say?' Sam asked.

'I said, "I do love you",' Mulberry said, gazing off into the distance. 'And I do, you know. Not being soppy or anything.'

Sam took a deep breath and wrapped her arms around Mulberry's neck.

'I didn't mean to hurt that little two-legs, neither,' said Mulberry. 'Honestly, I didn't see her.' Sam nodded and buried her face in Mulberry's thick mane, tears trickling down her face.

'I know,' Sam said.

They stood there like that for a moment saying nothing, Mulberry looking all around her as if trying to fix every sight and sound and smell in her memory.

Sam leaned her cheek against Mulberry's neck so she could look at her. 'You know Mulberry, if this works, you're going

to have to put up with me as a rider,'
Sam said.

'I could do that,' Mulberry said. 'I mean,
you're a bit rough around the edges and it

will take a bit of time to train you up but we'll get there in the end.'

Sam turned her face to hide her smile in Mulberry's mane. 'A bit rough around the edges' was high praise from Mulberry.

'I love you, Mulberry,' Sam said, squeezing the little mare so hard that Mulberry gasped. 'If I were your owner, I'd keep you safe. I'd make sure you had your favourite green apples every day and you'd never be hungry or cold or lonely.'

Mulberry nudged at Sam with her nose and when Sam turned her head to look at her, Mulberry licked her face.

'I know,' Mulberry said. 'This plan of yours is going to work, isn't it?'

Sam said nothing and simply pressed her lips against Mulberry's nose in a hard kiss. The plan *had* to work, it just had to.

Her heart hurt too much for her to think about what would happen if it didn't.

Mulberry whipped her head round to stare into the distance, arching her neck and pricking her ears. Sam couldn't hear anything unusual but Mulberry had much better hearing than she did.

'Is someone coming?' she asked.

'Yes!' Mulberry said. 'I can hear hoof beats coming from the direction of Meadow Vale. It must be the rescue party.'

'OK,' Sam said, butterflies taking flight in her stomach. 'Remember what we agreed and stick to the plan.'

'I have to be overcome with grief that you are injured,' Mulberry said.

'Exactly,' Sam said. 'And you are so upset that you cannot bear to leave me: all your protective instincts have kicked in and you think you have to take care of me yourself and you are worried about letting anyone else near me.'

Mulberry rolled her eyes. 'This sounds like a really bad book.'

'It doesn't matter!'

'Holes in the plot big enough to ride through on Velvet . . . '

'Fine, let's give up and go home then, shall we?' Sam snapped.

'I didn't say that, did I?' Mulberry said. 'Carry on.'

'Look, the important thing is, you have to make a scene and it has to look believable. You have to lie next to me and look upset and heartbroken and all that stuff.'

'You're really going for a shameless tug on the heartstrings, aren't you?'

'Whatever it takes.'

'OK then, get into position,' Mulberry said. Sam lay down on the ground and arranged her arms and legs the way they had been when Natalie had seen her fall off.

'I can hear an engine now,' Mulberry said, cocking her head. 'What do you think that is, an ambulance?'

Oh no! Sam had forgotten the stables would dial 999 straightaway once they heard she had fallen. So not only was she going to be lying to her mother but also to the emergency services. How much trouble would she get into for that? She was going to have to 'wake up' quickly before they realized she was only pretending to be out cold.

'Lie down, Mulberry,' Sam said. 'Look upset!'

'Right you are,' Mulberry said, and she stepped so close to Sam's head that Sam felt a puff of air against her face as the hoof slammed down into the grass.

'Watch where you're walking!' Sam said.

'Stop talking,' Mulberry whispered. 'They're coming!'

Sam tried to relax her whole body and keep her breathing slow and calm. She tried not flinch as Mulberry settled her bulk next to her and wrapped her body around Sam's. She laid her head on Sam's back.

Mulberry was certainly putting on a show. 'Oh woe, woe is me,' she moaned.

'What are you doing?' Sam whispered.

'Getting into character,' Mulberry said.

'Stop it!' Sam hissed.

Sam could hear the sound of voices now and the three-beat rhythm of horses cantering. 'Sam!' someone yelled. Sam recognized Amy's voice. She could hear an engine rumbling to a stop and the sound of car doors slamming. The voices grew quieter and Mulberry nudged at her with her nose before laying her head back down on top of Sam's still body. There was a conversation going on and Sam strained her ears to hear it.

'We have to get her moved soon,' said a man's voice. 'If she has hit her head, then we need to get her to hospital as fast as possible. She also needs to be strapped to a board in case she has hurt her back. If that pony doesn't let us get close to her then we are going to have to call a vet to come out here and drug it. But that's going to take time—we need to move her now. Is she going to get nasty with us if we try and move her away from your sister?'

'Um, normally, I would say yes but I've never seen this pony behave like this before,' Sam heard Amy say. 'I think she's just very upset. Let me try and move her. I know the pony, she might let me get near to her.'

Suddenly, Mulberry sprang to her feet and began to pace up and down in front of Sam, pawing the ground and whinnying with anxiety. Amy stepped back and Sam flinched at the mare's sudden movement.

'Sam! Are you OK?' Amy cried.

Hearing the worry in her sister's voice, Sam sat up, slowly. Mulberry bent her head down and nuzzled her hard.

'Why did you jump up? That wasn't the plan,' Sam whispered to Mulberry.

'It won't work,' Mulberry replied, her black eyes sparking with panic. 'They are never going to believe us!'

Sam reached out and folded her arms around Mulberry's head. 'You should have stuck to the plan,' Sam whispered in her ear, tears trickling down her face.

'You didn't see the look on Amy's face— she thinks I hurt you,' Mulberry said. 'They are never going to let us be together!'

Sam peeped over Mulberry's nose at Amy. All she saw was her sister looking worried. Mulberry must have assumed

Amy was angry. 'Oh, Mulberry,' she whispered. 'Amy has never thought you were a bad pony.'

Sam heard hoof beats and her mother's panicked voice but she held onto Mulberry as tight as she could, her tears sliding down Mulberry's cheeks. Why did they ever think this was going to work? They were never going to get away with lying to everyone.

As Mum dismounted from Velvet, Mulberry looked up and neighed so loudly her body vibrated. The neigh was full of grief and Sam saw Mum's eyes water as she reached for the dangling reins.

'Oh, Mulberry,' Mum said. 'Easy girl.' Mum clutched the reins and stroked Mulberry's neck with a slow, gentle hand. Mulberry bent her head to nuzzle Sam

again, nickering with distress. Sam cried
harder and clutched at Mulberry's face.

'Good girl, Mulberry, nice girl,' Mum
said. 'Be calm now, let us get to Sam, good
girl.' Mulberry shuddered as Mum clicked
her tongue and pulled on the reins, forcing
the reluctant pony away from Sam. She
whinnied pitifully and pawed the ground
as she was led away.

'I'm fine,' Sam said, as the paramedics
examined her and then she was lifted up
by two pairs of hands and laid down on a

hard, rigid board. 'Really, I'm fine, I just slipped off in canter.'

'Standard procedure in a riding accident, I'm afraid,' said one of the ambulance men, smiling down at her. 'We have to get you to a hospital and get you checked out, especially if you had a bump on the head.'

'But I didn't hit my head!' Sam said.

'Let's get her into hospital as fast as we can,' said the paramedic to his companion, ignoring Sam. 'Radio ahead and tell A&E we have a riding accident on the way.'

She was lifted into the air on the board and carried to the ambulance. Mum was asking someone to take Mulberry back to the stables because she wanted to go in the ambulance with Sam. The ambulance doors were being slammed again and the noise outside was muffled.

'It's all a mistake,' Sam said, trying to sit up.

'Shush,' Mum soothed, stroking her forehead with cool hands. Sam could smell horse and leather and saddle soap when her Mum bent to kiss her cheek. Strapped to the board, Sam cried as Mulberry called and called for her over the noise of the ambulance pulling away. Clutched tight in Sam's fist were a few long strands of mane that had caught in her fingers when Mulberry had been pulled away. Instead of Mulberry staying calm and looking like she was protecting Sam, she had panicked. Sam looked at her mum. Would she see that Mulberry had just been worried that they would be separated? Sam scrunched her eyes closed. Their plan had failed.

Chapter 13

Once they got to A&E, the nurses had insisted on keeping Sam strapped to the horrible board until a doctor had seen her. It was torture! Sam literally couldn't move a muscle and her whole body began to ache with the strain. She hadn't realized that not being able to move would hurt! She longed to turn her head and roll onto her side, but the most she could do was wiggle her fingers and toes. She began to panic, just a little, at the feeling of being trapped. Fear rose like a bubble from her stomach and then lodged in her throat, making her feel as if she couldn't breathe.

A hot, prickly sweat broke out over her whole body and she whimpered.

Mum leaned over her. 'Are you OK?' she asked, her green eyes full of worry.

'I'm fine,' Sam said. 'I just want to get off this thing!'

'What happened back there?'

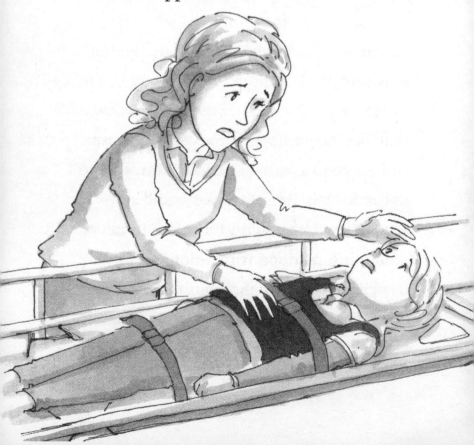

'I slipped off,' Sam said. 'That's all that happened; Mulberry didn't hurt me!'

'I can see that,' Mum said. 'You're wriggling around like a bag of monkeys!'

'Please don't let her be sold to someone else Mum, I can't bear to be apart from her!'

'Sam . . . '

'And she can't bear to be apart from me!' Sam said.

Mum sighed. 'Yes, I can see that.'

'We're bonded Mum, just like you and Velvet,' Sam said.

'It's not that simple,' Mum said.

'Why not?' Sam asked, beginning to cry again with fear and frustration.

'Riding can be dangerous, Sam,' Mum said. 'Horses and ponies are big animals and you can get hurt. My job is to protect you and even though I ride myself and I love it too, when I watch you ride I feel sick with nerves in case you fall off.' Mum smiled. 'Sometimes, I wish you didn't ride. But if you do, I want it to be on the safest pony I can find.'

'But that's silly!' Sam said.

'I know, but that's what it's like being a Mum.'

Sam thought for a second. 'Do you feel the same way when you ride?'

'No,' Mum laughed.

'Why not?'

'Because I trust Velvet completely and I trust myself.'

'Well, I trust Mulberry the way you trust Velvet,' Sam said. 'She makes me feel confident. Apart from Velvet, she's the only animal I have ever ridden that makes me feel so safe. You need to listen to me, Mum, and you need to trust me too. You know she loves me. And she has never misbehaved with me.'

Mum sighed. 'Come on, Sam, you know that's not strictly true. Mulberry can be a naughty pony. But I saw how she stayed with you. The way you looked at each other reminded me of Velvet and me.'

'She's the only pony for me and I'm the only rider for her,' Sam said. 'Please Mum, she's my Velvet.'

Mum's eyes softened and she stroked Sam's cheek. 'Oh, Sam,' she said.

By the time Amy and Miss Mildew arrived at the hospital, the doctor had declared Sam to be just fine. Now they were just waiting to be discharged. It was a relief to Sam's aching muscles, which had taken enough punishment that day.

Miss Mildew walked up to Sam's bed, a very stiff, uncomfortable smile perched on her face. 'I just came to see how the patient was doing,' she said. Miss Mildew shook her head. 'I did warn you, Miss Grey, that your poor riding skills on such a naughty pony could lead to an accident. I'm sorry you persuaded me to let you ride Mulberry today. The sooner that mare is gone, the better.'

'About that,' Mum said with a sigh. 'Sam is very fond of Mulberry and wants me to buy her. If she continues to behave for Sam the way she did at the Summer Show and she protects her when they are on their own, then I think I might be persuaded that Mulberry is the pony for her.'

Sam looked up at her mother, a smile breaking like sunshine over her face. 'Do you mean that? Really?!'

'I must be mad,' Mum said, a small smile tugging at her lips. 'But Mulberry didn't hurt you and the pair of you do seem to

have bonded. And what kind of mother would I be if I broke your heart?'

Sam threw her arms around her mother's waist and squeezed her so hard she couldn't breathe. 'Let go or I might change my mind!' Mum said, laughing, while Amy jumped up and down on the spot with joy.

'Well, this is good news!' Miss Mildew said, a real smile on her face now as she thought of the money she was going to make. 'As you know, the asking price for Mulberry is £1,500, how would you like to pay?'

£1,500? That was ten times more than Sam had in her bank account. She couldn't afford to buy Mulberry!

'Please Miss Mildew, I've only got £100 and . . . ' She looked at her Mum.

'50,' Mum said.

'. . . £150 in my bank account,' Sam said. 'I know it isn't the full asking price . . . '

'It's nowhere near!' Miss Mildew said.

'. . . but I will work for free at the weekends . . . '

'You already do!' Miss Mildew said.

'And I will be paying livery to keep Mulberry at Meadow Vale,' Mum said. 'What I will pay in livery fees in one year will be more than a £1,000 anyway. It really is a very good deal for a pony you were happy to give away yesterday, just to be shot of her. The pony will now earn you money rather than being a burden.'

'This really is most unusual,' Miss Mildew said.

'It is,' Mum agreed. 'But Sam has her heart set on Mulberry. A pony is only worth what someone is willing to pay for it and Sam is willing to spend everything she has to own her.'

'I'm really not sure I want the responsibility of anything happening to Sam while riding Mulberry,' Miss Mildew said.

'But Miss Mildew, Mulberry is really good with me, it was my fault I fell off,' Sam said.

'Well, perhaps you should have more lessons then,' Miss Mildew said, looking a little more cheerful. Sam flicked a quick glance towards Mum and could see her desperately trying not to roll her eyes. 'Perhaps with some more tuition you would both be a safer combination.'

'So will you sell her to me, please?' Sam asked, trying not to sound too desperate.

She held her breath and slipped a hand under the sheets, crossing her fingers for luck.

Miss Mildew looked at Mum. 'Her livery bill will be paid for every month, on time?'

Mum narrowed her eyes. 'Of course, as is Velvet's.'

Miss Mildew sighed irritably. 'Fine, I will accept your offer, even though it is much lower than I originally wanted. You're getting a bargain, Miss Grey.'

'So are you, Miss Mildew,' Mum said. 'I shall write you a cheque for the full amount right now; Sam can pay me back later. I have a pen and paper so you can write Sam a receipt.'

A muscle in Miss Mildew's jaw jumped as she clenched it tight but she said nothing, took the pen and paper from

Mum and scribbled something down, before handing it to Sam.

'Congratulations on the purchase of your first pony,' Miss Mildew said stiffly, her face grim. 'I wish you joy of her.'

'How nice,' Mum said. 'Now, shall we let Sam get a bit of rest while I speak to the doctor?' And with that Mum steered Miss Mildew away.

As they walked down the corridor, Sam looked after them, her brain trying to understand what had just happened. Amy leaned down and smoothed the crumpled piece of paper lying in Sam's lap.

'You did it, Sam,' she said, her eyes shining with happiness for her sister. 'You really did it. You own Mulberry.'

Still in shock, Sam took the paper from

Amy's hand and read what it said, over and over again until it sunk in.

Sold by Miss Mildew

to Samantha Grey,

for the sum of £150,

one vile black pony,

breed unknown,

by the name of Mulberry.

A Mildew

Chapter 14

Although Sam was let out of hospital the same day, Mum insisted on her staying at home in bed for another day, while she fussed over her. She wanted to make sure Sam was fully recovered before she let her go to the stables. 'If I so much as see you wince,' she warned, 'you won't be riding for a month, new pony or not.'

Sam was in a fever of excitement and the car seemed to move so slowly when Mum finally agreed they could drive to the yard. It seemed every traffic light was red, every zebra crossing had herds of people wanting to cross, and when they

167

finally got out into the countryside and found themselves stuck behind a very slow tractor, Sam could have torn her hair out with frustration.

'Calm down!' Mum said, laughing at Sam's reflection in the rear-view mirror as the car crawled along behind the tractor at ten miles an hour. 'Mulberry isn't going anywhere.'

When they finally got to Meadow Vale Stables, Sam nearly broke the door handle off the car in her haste to get out. She slammed the door and ran off through the yard, legs practically blurring as she raced towards Mulberry's stable on the bottom yard. She heard Mum and Amy shouting and laughing behind her but she was too giddy with happiness to listen or to stop.

'Mulberry, Mulberry have you heard?'

she called as she ran through the archway into the cool calm of the bottom yard. There was no black head hanging over the door to see her, no welcoming neigh. Sam's steps slowed to a walk and a horrible thought crossed her mind. Has Mulberry gone? Did someone change their mind and buy her anyway for £1,500? Was Miss Mildew going to hand her money back with a shrug and tell her she had to take the higher offer for the 'perfect' home? She clenched her sweaty hands into fists and almost fainted with relief as Mulberry popped her head over the door and made a rumbling noise in her throat.

Sam grinned at her, excitement bubbling up again. 'Haven't you heard?' she asked.

'Heard what?' Mulberry asked.

'Mum changed her mind!' Sam said.

'I'm your owner now!'

'Oh that,' Mulberry said. 'Yeah, I heard.'

'Well? Aren't you happy?' Sam asked.

'Oh yeah,' Mulberry said. 'Overjoyed. My cup runneth over.'

Mulberry seemed to be determined to be her normal, grumpy, ungrateful self but

Sam was so happy, she just didn't care. She slid back the bolts on Mulberry's stable door and threw herself at the little black mare, wrapping her arms around her neck and squeezing her as hard as she could.

'You're not going to cry are you?' Mulberry asked. 'I hate it when you leak.'

'Don't be so grumpy, Mulberry,' Sam said, rubbing Mulberry's long nose. 'I know you love me.'

Mulberry snorted. 'I was acting, getting into character,' she said. 'I got caught up in the moment, that's all.'

Sam laughed. 'You are such a bad liar,' she buried her face in Mulberry's mane. 'I love you, Mulberry.'

'Love you more,' the mare said, quietly.

'It's not a competition,' Sam said.

'If it was, you'd lose,' Mulberry said.

'No one beats me at anything.'

'You'd better take care of her,' said a rich, warm voice behind them.

Sam whirled to see Velvet standing outside the stable—she had been so wrapped up in Mulberry Sam hadn't heard the mare walking across the flagstones of the bottom yard. Sam flew out of the door and wrapped her arms around Velvet's muscly, glossy black neck. She sighed with happiness as Velvet dipped her head down and cuddled Sam against her broad chest, her whole body vibrating as she rumbled in her throat.

'I am so glad you're not hurt,' Velvet said. She looked at Mulberry. 'And I am so glad you didn't live up to your reputation and stayed by her. Keep it up. The safest place in the world for Sam had better be on your back or I won't be pleased.'

Mulberry moved towards the sunlit door, her eyes gleaming. ''Course,' she said. 'I mind my riders.'

Velvet snorted as Amy came running up, red-faced and out of breath. 'Here she is,' she said. 'Sorry, Sam, I left her stable for a second to get her some hay and she must have nudged the door open behind me and walked off! I ran up to the fields looking for her, I never thought she would ignore all the grazing just for a mooch around the yard.'

Velvet gave Sam one last nuzzle with her soft nose before Amy clipped a lead rope to her head collar and led her away.

'Well, that was touching,' Mulberry said. 'Get me an apple, would you? A nice tart green apple. You promised—you said that if you became my owner I'd get an apple every day. Well, you've been an owner for two days now, two and a half if we count that day in the hospital (which I am) and I haven't seen a single apple yet. So get a move on and fetch me some. Chop, chop!'

'Hang on a second, Mulberry,' Sam said, laughing. 'Work first, then you get a treat.'

'That wasn't our deal!' Mulberry said.

'There was no deal,' Sam said. 'Now stop being so grumpy! I'm your owner now, you can't boss me around like you used to.'

'We'll see about that,' Mulberry said, as Sam went off to the tack room to fetch Mulberry's saddle and bridle.

Sam was so light with happiness, she felt she could have floated onto Mulberry's back. She trotted Mulberry through the yard, smiling and nodding as other liveries called out their congratulations. Every face that turned towards them was smiling to see Sam so happy, and Sam felt as if the ground should have been strewn with rose petals so Mulberry could have trotted on a red carpet. Mulberry arched her neck and bounced from hoof to hoof with pride, her chest puffed out. A couple of liveries offered to come riding with Sam but she smiled and shook her head. Today, right now, it was just going to be her and Mulberry. The Shetlands lifted their heads as she went past but kept their insults to themselves, and Basil nodded his head at them. Amy waved as she led Velvet back to her stable. The big black cob gave Mulberry such a hard look of warning that she sped up to get past her.

But Sam and Mulberry did stop for Minnie. 'Thank you,' Sam said, while Mulberry rubbed noses with her.

'You're welcome, two-legs,' Minnie said as she shuffled off. 'Any time you need advice, you know where I am. I'm also available for after-dinner speaking, weddings, and Bar Mitzvahs.'

When they set hoof on the bridle path that led from Meadow Vale to the woods, Sam leaned down and patted Mulberry on the neck. The little mare snorted and bounced with excitement.

'Are you ready to have some fun?' Sam asked.

In answer, Mulberry bounded forward and galloped towards the trees. Sam stood up in the stirrups and bent low over Mulberry's neck like a racing jockey, the

mare's thick black mane whipping towards her face, and the wind roaring in her ears and drowning out all other sounds except for the steady beat of Mulberry's hoofs. Sam grinned as the wind whipped tears from her eyes and everyone on the yard, two-legs, pony and horse, looked up at the sound of Sam whooping and Mulberry neighing for the sheer joy of being alive and together!

MEET THE PONIES!

Mulberry

BREED: Exmoor X Welsh. Both Welsh and Exmoor ponies are native British breeds. Both breeds are renowned for being intelligent, which Mulberry definitely is—and she knows it, too! Welsh ponies are often very spirited and lively, like Mulberry, whereas Exmoor ponies tend to have kinder and gentler temperaments. Both breeds are very strong despite their small size, and are tough enough to live outside all year round.

HEIGHT: 12.2hh (a 'hand' is 4 inches. So Mulberry is 12 and a half hands high.)

COLOUR: Jet black   **MARKINGS:** None

FAVOURITE FOOD: Green apples (no bruised ones though—only the very best for this special pony!)

LIKES: Showing off, going fast, and being scratched behind the ears.

DISLIKES: Rain, bruised apples, and hippo-faced Shetland ponies.

Velvet

BREED: Irish cob. Irish cobs are very sure-footed—making them really safe and comfortable to ride. They're exceptionally kind, very intelligent, and are big and strong, just like Velvet. Perfect for cuddles!

HEIGHT: 15.2hh

COLOUR: Black

MARKINGS: White star in between her eyes that looks like a big diamond.

FAVOURITE FOOD: Any treats, but especially carrots.

LIKES: Hugs, hay, and being taken out for rides.

DISLIKES: Naughty little ponies.

Apricot

BREED: Miniature Shetland pony. Shetland ponies originally come from the Shetland Islands in the very north of Scotland, although they're now found all over the world. Although they're the smallest native British breed, they're also the strongest (for their size). They are really brave, and tend to have very strong characters—which explains Apricot's feisty personality!

HEIGHT: 9hh

COLOUR: Dun with flaxen mane and tail. Dun is a warm shade of brown—like the colour of an apricot, and having a flaxen mane and tail is like having blonde hair.

MARKINGS: None

FAVOURITE FOOD: Hay, and lots of it!

LIKES: Making mischief and getting away with it!

DISLIKES: When Basil comes too close to the fence.

PONY-MAD QUIZ!

Do you know your manes from your tails and your body brushes from your hoof picks? Do our **MEADOW VALE QUIZ** to find out if you're a pony whiz!

1 What kind of pony is Mulberry?
- **a.** Shetland pony
- **b.** Exmoor X Welsh pony
- **c.** Highland pony

2 What is a pony's height measured in?
- **a.** Fingers
- **b.** Hoofs
- **c.** Hands

3 Where on a pony might you find a star?
- **a.** Their face
- **b.** Their legs
- **c.** Under their tail

4 What colour is a piebald horse?
- **a.** Brown
- **b.** Black and white
- **c.** Brown and white

5 What are the best clothes for horse riding?

   a. Pyjamas

   b. Jeans and flip-flops

   c. Jodhpurs and boots with a small heel

6 If you're told to groom your pony, what would you do?

   a. Use brushes to clean your pony all over

   b. Feed your pony a carrot

   c. Put your pony away in its stable

7 What would you use a hoof pick for?

   a. Filling in holes made by hoofs

   b. Making your pony's mane shine

   c. Picking out (and cleaning) your pony's hoofs

8 What is it called when you clean your pony's stable?

   a. Mucking out

   b. Mucking in

   c. Scrubbing up

9 What is a forelock?

   a. A type of padlock used for ponies' stables

   b. The front part of a pony's mane

   c. A part of a pony's front leg

10 Where would you put a pony's bit when getting ready to ride?

a. On their hoofs

b. Under their saddle

c. In their mouth

11 From slowest to fastest, what is the correct order of a pony's paces?

a. Gallop, canter, walk, trot

b. Walk, trot, canter, gallop

c. Walk, canter, gallop, trot

12 What is the name of Sam's riding instructor?

a. Miss Mildew

b. Minnie the Moocher

c. Natalie

13 How is a pony feeling if its ears are back?

a. Happy, friendly, and playful

b. Angry, annoyed, or scared

c. Sleepy

14 Who does Apricot share her part of the barn with?

a. Velvet

b. Mulberry

c. Turbo and Mickey

15 What is a baby pony called?

    a. A foal

    b. A pup

    c. A duckling

ANSWERS

1. b; 2. c; 3. a; 4. b; 5. c; 6. a; 7. c; 8. a; 9. b; 10 c; 11. b; 12. a; 13. b; 14. c; 15. a

RESULTS

0-4 correct: Uh oh! Are you getting your ponies confused with your penguins? Read *Mulberry for Sale* again and have another go. You can also learn a lot about ponies from books and magazines—have a look in the non-fiction section of your local library. Keep trying!

5-10 correct: You know the basics and are on your way to becoming a pony expert—well done! Keep reading books and magazines, and spend as much time around horses and ponies as possible. You'll be a pony whiz in no time!

11-15 correct: You deserve a big rosette for being so clever about horses and ponies. There's always more to learn though, so keep up the good work and enjoy being a pony superstar!

ABOUT THE AUTHOR!

CHE GOLDEN is a graduate of the Masters course in Creative Writing for Young People at Bath Spa University. *The Meadow Vale Ponies* series are her first books for Oxford University Press.

Che's first horse was Velvet, a huge, black Irish cob who not only taught Che how to ride, but taught her two little girls as well. Now, they own Charlie Brown, a rather neurotic New Forest pony, and Robbie, a very laid-back Highland pony. Mulberry is based on a little black mare, Brie, who Che's daughter fell in love with, despite the fact that Brie managed to terrorize a yard of 50 horses and vets wanted danger money to go anywhere near her.

Che also has two pet ferrets, Mike and Mindy, and a Manchester Terrier called Beau Nash.